WILBUR SMITH

The Diamond Hunters

Retold by Margaret Tarner

Series Editor: John Milne

The Heinemann ELT Guided Readers provide a choice of enjoyable reading material for learners of English. The series is published at five levels – Starter, Beginner, Elementary, Intermediate and Upper. At **Intermediate Level**, the control of content and language has the following main features:

Information Control

Information which is vital to the understanding of the story is presented in an easily assimilated manner and is repeated when necessary. Difficult allusion and metaphor are avoided and cultural backgrounds are made explicit.

Structure Control

Most of the structures used in the Readers will be familiar to students who have completed an elementary course of English. Other grammatical features may occur, but their use is made clear through context and reinforcement. This ensures that the reading, as well as being enjoyable, provides a continual learning situation for the students. Sentences are limited in most cases to a maximum of three clauses and within sentences there is a balanced use of simple adverbial and adjectival phrases. Great care is taken with pronoun reference.

Vocabulary Control

There is a basic vocabulary of approximately 1,600 words. Help is given to the students in the form of illustrations which are closely related to the text.

Glossary

Some difficult words and phrases in this book are important for understanding the story. Some of these words are explained in the story, some are shown in the pictures, and others are marked with a number like this ...[3] Words with a number are explained in the Glossary on page 71.

Contents

The People in This Story

Jacobus Van Der Byl (the 'Old Man')
Father of Benedict and Tracey. The Old Man started the Van Der Byl Diamond Company. He is old and very rich. He lives in a large house in Cape Town, South Africa.

Benedict Van Der Byl
Son of Jacobus van der Byl. Benedict is a director of Van Der Byl Diamond Company. He likes to spend money and enjoy himself. He has always hated Johnny Lance.

Tracey Van Der Byl
Daughter of Jacobus van der Byl. Tracey is a director of Van Der Byl Diamond Company. Tracey is in love with Johnny Lance.

Johnny Lance
A director of the Van Der Byl Diamond
Company. Jacobus van der Byl found
Johnny when he was a small boy. Johnny
had no family and he was poor. The Old
Man called Johnny his son. He educated
him and gave him a job in the mining
company. Johnny is married to Ruby
Lance but he loves Tracey van der Byl.

Ruby Lance
Wife of Johnny Lance. Ruby is a
beautiful but hard woman. She does not
love Johnny now, but she will not
divorce him.

Hugo Kramer
The German captain of the fishing boat,
Wild Goose.

Sergio Caporetti
The Italian captain of the dredging ship, *Kingfisher*.

Kaminikoto
The Japanese computer expert.

Mr Larsen
The head of Larsen Finance Company. He lends money to Van Der Byl Diamond Company so *Kingfisher* can be built.

1

The Old Man's Will

The Old Man sat in the chair. His face was very white. He stared at the doctor.

'Can you do anything?' he asked.

The doctor shook his head.

'Then how long have I got?'

'Six months, not more,' the doctor replied.

'Are you sure?'

'Yes.'

Jacobus van der Byl, the Old Man, stood up slowly.

'Then I have some things to do,' he said.

The Old Man went home to his big house and phoned his lawyers[1].

'I want to add something to my will[2],' he told them. 'Send someone to the house immediately.'

When the lawyer had left, the Old Man sat alone in his study[3]. He stood up and walked to the cupboard where he kept his guns. Jacobus van der Byl had decided not to wait for death to come to him. He took out his gun and shot himself through the mouth. He died – as he had lived – alone.

Strong winds were blowing clouds over Table Mountain. As the sun went down, the sky over Cape Town turned a clear orange.

A tall man stood staring out of the window. He had broad shoulders and a hard, strong body.

The lawyer began to speak. The tall man, whose name was Johnny Lance, turned to face the others – Tracey and Benedict

Jacobus van der Byl had decided not to wait for death to come to him.

van der Byl. Two people he had known all his life. One he loved. The other hated him.

'As you all know,' the lawyer said, 'the Van Der Byl Diamond Company is in trouble. There are debts[4], big debts. And there is very little money left. In his last will, Jacobus van der Byl made you – Tracey and Benedict van der Byl, his children, and you, Johnny Lance – directors of the company.'

Johnny took a step forward. A director of Van Der Byl Diamonds? He could not believe it. He had always thought that the Old Man had hated him. Perhaps the Old Man had not hated him.

Johnny looked at Tracey and they both smiled.

'I'm so glad, Johnny, so glad,' Tracey whispered[5]. Her beautiful, dark eyes were full of tears. Then Johnny looked at Benedict. The handsome young man was not smiling.

'There is something else,' the lawyer went on. He began reading from the will.

'I, Jacobus van der Byl, also make John Rigby Lance personally responsible[6] for all the debts of Van Der Byl Diamonds.'

'Personally responsible for all the debts?' said Johnny. 'But why?'

Benedict leant forward. He was now smiling.

'I can tell you why,' Benedict said. 'The Old Man hated you for doing better than me – his own son. He hated you for the way you looked at Tracey, my pretty little sister.

'You were a poor little boy when the Old Man took you into his house. He was sorry for you then and he gave you everything. But that's all changed. He's ruined[7] you, Johnny. You were born poor and you'll die poor. Now you have debts of two and a half million rand[8]. How do you like that?'

'But it's crazy. Two and a half million rand!' Johnny shouted. 'I haven't got ten thousand rand! Everyone knows that. Who would try to get the money from me?'

'I would, Johnny,' Benedict said. 'I'll be happy to take your last penny.'

'But why?' Johnny asked again.

'I've told you why,' Benedict replied. 'You've always done better than me – in sport, in business, even with women. But now, at last, I can beat you.'

Benedict stood up and the two men stared at each other. Both were tall and dark, with broad shoulders. Johnny's face was hard, browned by the South African sun. But Benedict's handsome face was pale and weak.

Then Johnny smiled. 'I will find more diamonds,' he said.

'And where are you going to find more diamonds?' asked Benedict. 'There are no more diamonds left in our concession[9]. There are no more diamonds in the mines.'

'I have the ship. I have *Kingfisher*,' said Johnny. 'I am going to search the sea for diamonds. I know that there are diamonds at the bottom of the sea.'

'*Kingfisher*! That crazy ship?' Benedict laughed. '*Kingfisher* is in England. The ship is still being built. Johnny, you're beaten!'

'No, I'm not,' replied Johnny. 'I've got *Kingfisher*. I've designed the equipment[10] myself. If there are diamonds to be found, I'll find them.'

Benedict laughed. 'I'm going to London,' he said. 'I've got business to do there.'

He walked out of the room.

The lawyer picked up his papers and left the room. Johnny and Tracey were left alone together. They stood looking at each other.

'Johnny, I'm sorry,' said Tracey. But Johnny was smiling now.

'Tracey,' he said. 'I'm flying up to the company concession at Cartridge Bay tomorrow. Will you come with me?'

2

Thunderbolt and Suicide

The following morning, the company plane took off from Cape Town. Johnny was flying the plane and Tracey was sitting beside him.

They both felt excited. Johnny was sure that they would be able to use *Kingfisher* to find diamonds. He was going to save the company. Tracey believed him.

'When will *Kingfisher* be ready?' Tracey asked.

'It should be ready to leave England in three weeks' time,' Johnny said. 'I've found a captain for *Kingfisher*. He'll fly to England and sail *Kingfisher* back to Cartridge Bay.'

'Who is the captain?' asked Tracey.

'The best,' Johnny answered. 'His name's Sergio Caporetti. He's Italian and he's done work like this before. He's very good at his job.'

'But Van Der Byl have looked for diamonds off-shore[11] before,' Tracey said. 'They never found any.'

'But we've got *Kingfisher* now,' Johnny answered. 'I am sure we will find diamonds when we use *Kingfisher*.'

They had been flying for four hours. Now Johnny crossed the coast[12] and turned the plane out to sea.

'Now I want to show you something else, Tracey,' he said. 'Look down there, at those two islands.'

Tracey looked down. The plane was now flying low over the sea.

'Those two lumps of white rock are called Thunderbolt and Suicide,' Johnny said. 'Look at their shape. They are both very narrow – they are only four kilometres long. Can you see the small gap[13] between them? Can you see how the sea rushes through that gap?'

'What a terrible place,' Tracey said quietly. 'If a ship got too near those islands it would be smashed to pieces.'

'I agree it's a dangerous place,' said Johnny. 'But listen. I've been working with diamonds all my life. I can smell them. I know there are diamonds down there. The gap between those two islands is a diamond trap. Diamonds were washed into the gap millions of years ago. I know there are diamonds down there under fifty metres of water. And I'm the only one who knows it.'

'And with *Kingfisher*, you can get them out,' Tracey said, her eyes shining.

'Yes, but there's one problem,' said Johnny. 'Thunderbolt and Suicide are not part of our concession. I know there are diamonds down there – big, marvellous[14] diamonds! But they don't belong to us. They belong to the government. We can't touch them.' And Johnny turned the plane back towards the land.

'Look, there's Cartridge Bay,' Tracey said a few minutes later.

'OK. Down we go,' said Johnny. 'We'll have lunch, look round the concession and then fly back to Cape Town.'

———

Hugo Kramer, captain of the fishing boat, *Wild Goose*, watched the plane flying towards Cape Town. At first he had thought it was a police patrol[15]. But then he saw the company sign. It was a Van Der Byl plane. Hugo Kramer was safe.

Hugo Kramer was afraid of police patrols. He was a pilchard[16] fisherman – but he was also a diamond smuggler.

———

Diamond smuggling was dangerous. If you were caught, you were

12

'I know there are diamonds down there.'

put in prison for fifteen years. But if you were not caught, you made a lot of money. You made much more money smuggling diamonds than fishing for pilchards.

Hugo Kramer was waiting for the sun to go down. When it was dark, a balloon would come down from the sky. It would fall in the sea near the *Wild Goose*. Hugo Kramer was waiting for that balloon.

There was a large diamond mine far away in the desert. A security officer[17] who worked in the mine was also a diamond smuggler. The security officer stole the diamonds and sent them to Hugo Kramer. It was easy. The security officer put the diamonds in a metal box. He tied the box to a gas-filled[18] balloon. The balloon flew up in the air. The wind blew the balloon over the desert and out over the sea.

It was night. On the *Wild Goose*, Hugo Kramer was watching the radar screen[19]. Then, suddenly, a light came onto the screen. It was the balloon. The strong winds had blown the balloon across the desert. And now it was coming down into the sea, just in the right place.

Kramer ran up onto the deck[20].

'Turn on the lights!' he shouted.

One of the crewmen turned on the lights. They shone on the metal box tied to the balloon floating on the water. When the balloon was on board, Kramer took the box to his cabin[21]. He locked the door.

Diamonds! Twenty-seven large, beautiful diamonds! Kramer had to work quickly. He put the diamonds into a tin can. Then he filled the tin can with hot wax[22]. When the wax was cold, he closed the can tightly.

Kramer stuck a label round the tin. It said: "Pilchards in Tomato Sauce. Van Dee Bee Agencies, South Africa". Kramer

14

Diamonds! Twenty-seven large, beautiful diamonds!

laughed. No one would know that this can had diamonds in it not pilchards. Kramer put the tin can in his jacket pocket.

Wild Goose arrived at Cartridge Bay three hours later. Kramer left the boat and walked into the office of the canning factory. Kramer hung up his jacket and left the room. When he returned, his jacket pocket was empty. Hugo Kramer smiled to himself. The can of diamonds was already on its way to London.

3

Benedict Goes to London

Johnny looked at the postcard on his office desk. It was from his wife, Ruby. She was in London. She was spending money that Johnny did not have. A beautiful woman, but hard, Johnny thought, like a diamond. Why had he married her? He knew now that he had made a bad mistake.

For a moment, Johnny thought about Tracey. She too had made a bad marriage which had ended in divorce[23]. Where was Tracey? She had not been in the office for days.

There was a knock at the door. It opened and a fat young man came into the room. It was the Italian – Sergio Caporetti – the captain of *Kingfisher*.

'Hello, Sergio,' Johnny said. 'Sit down.'

'So, at last we are ready,' Sergio said. 'Three months I've been waiting, with nothing to do but grow fat!'

'*Kingfisher* is ready,' said Johnny. 'You and the crew are to fly to England as soon as possible. Then you will bring her back here. She's a beautiful ship.'

The two men talked about plans for the next hour and then Sergio left. Johnny worked late and, after a meal, drove home to his empty house.

Johnny woke up suddenly. It was two o'clock in the morning. The doorbell rang again. The bell rang and rang.

As Johnny opened the door, Tracey rushed in, shouting, 'Johnny! Johnny! I've got them. Both of them. They're yours!'

'What do you mean? Where have you been?' Johnny asked.

'Sit down and don't ask questions,' Tracey said. 'I have some wonderful news. You won't believe it.'

'Believe what?'

'No questions, please.'

Johnny sat down and Tracey opened her briefcase[24]. She took out some papers and threw them down on the table.

'First, this is the old concession for Thunderbolt and Suicide. It belonged to a little company in Windhoek. The government didn't do anything about the concession because it was too small. Well, that's where I've been, Johnny, to Windhoek. And I . . .'

'You didn't . . .' Johnny began.

'Yes, I did. The owners of the concession think it's worth nothing. I gave them twenty thousand rand for it. They were delighted[25]. Here are the papers. Thunderbolt and Suicide are ours!'

'Tracey,' Johnny said, 'you're wonderful!'

Then he stood up and, suddenly, Tracey was in his arms.

The Managing Director of Van Dee Bee Agencies, London, took a can of pilchards out of his safe[26].

'This arrived yesterday,' he said.

Benedict van der Byl smiled when he saw the picture of the fish on the can. It was the can that Hugo Kramer had left in the canning factory at Cartridge Bay.

'Thank you,' Benedict said, putting the can into his briefcase. He left the Agency and drove through the busy streets of London to his flat. An hour later, he was standing outside an old building in Soho – in the centre of London.

Benedict rang a bell. Someone looked through a small window in the door. The door opened at once.

'Hello, Mr van der Byl,' a young man said. 'Come in.'

Benedict walked through a long room where some young men were hard at work. They were cutting diamonds.

The old man stood up as Benedict walked into his office.

'Benedict, my friend,' he said, holding out his hand. 'Welcome back to London.'

When the door was shut, Benedict took an envelope out of his pocket. He emptied it onto the desk.

'What do you think of these?' Benedict asked.

The man stared at the twenty-seven diamonds on his desk.

'Beautiful, beautiful,' he whispered.

The old man examined each one carefully, weighed them and then locked them in his safe.

'I'm a rich man now,' Benedict said. 'I'll make one or two more visits and that will be the end.'

The old man nodded sadly. 'I understand,' he said.

———

At midday, Benedict was back in his flat. The telephone rang and he answered it.

'Van der Byl,' he said and then his voice changed.

'What are you doing here? What a surprise! I thought you were in Paris. We must have lunch together. Where are you staying? Right. I'll meet you in the bar at one-fifteen. OK? See you then.'

Benedict had a shower and dressed carefully.

'This is going to be a great day!' he said to himself as he left the flat.

Benedict was in the bar first. He watched the beautiful blonde[27] coming towards him. Every other man in the room was looking at her too.

'Hello, Benedict,' she said.

'Ruby – Ruby Lance!' said Benedict. 'You look marvellous. It's good to see you again.'

That night, they went to the theatre. Then they went to a party. Ruby, with her long, fair hair and slim legs, was the most beautiful woman there.

But that was not why Benedict had decided to marry her. Ruby belonged to Johnny Lance. And what Johnny had, Benedict wanted.

4

'He Beats Me Every Time'

Benedict and Ruby met again the following evening. When Benedict saw Ruby, he kissed her and led her to his big, powerful car. As they drove through the busy London streets, Ruby thought about everything she was going to say and do.

Ruby knew that Benedict van der Byl was rich, very rich. He was much richer than Ruby's husband, Johnny Lance. Benedict could buy her diamonds. He could buy her beautiful clothes, take her to the best restaurants. Yes, Ruby decided that she wanted Benedict. But she knew she had to be careful. If she made one mistake, she would lose Benedict.

Benedict stopped the car outside his flat. Without speaking, Benedict led Ruby inside and sat her down in a chair. Ruby looked around her. The furniture was beautiful and there were expensive paintings on the walls. This was the home of a very rich man who loved beautiful things. Ruby smiled.

Then suddenly, Benedict began to talk. And he said everything that Ruby wanted to hear.

'Divorce Johnny quickly,' Benedict told her. 'I want you, Ruby. I've always wanted you. You are too good for Johnny. He has always tried to beat me. But now I'm going to ruin him.

'But I must be there when you tell him you want a divorce,' Benedict went on. 'Promise me. He must know that I am taking you away from him. Do you understand?'

Ruby nodded. She understood everything. Benedict wanted her because she belonged to Johnny Lance.

'Do you agree?' Benedict asked.

'Yes, I do,' Ruby answered.

'Then come in here. I have something to show you.'

Benedict led her into the bedroom. On the bed was a beautiful fur coat.

'My wife must wear only the best,' Benedict said. 'Put it on.'

Ruby walked to the bed in a dream. She tried on the coat. Benedict watched her. His handsome face was excited.

Ruby turned and smiled at him. The beautiful fur coat shone like silver.

'It's marvellous,' she said.

Benedict stood up and walked towards her.

'And now I have you,' he said and took Ruby in his arms.

Next day, they went shopping and Ruby wore her new fur coat. Everyone looked at her and Benedict was delighted.

'The wife of a diamond man must wear diamonds,' he said.

Then Benedict took Ruby to the old building in Soho. There he bought her two large diamonds. He paid twenty thousand pounds for them.

'We'll have them made into earrings,' said Benedict. 'Now

*Ruby turned and smiled at him The beautiful fur coat
shone like silver.*

it's time for lunch. But first, I want to read the newspapers from home.' Benedict drove to South Africa House[28] and picked up the South African newspapers. As soon as he saw the front page of the *Cape Argus*, his face changed.

'What's the matter?' Ruby asked.

Benedict gave her the paper and she read the headline: VAN DER BYL DIAMONDS WIN VALUABLE CONCESSION. LANCE GETS THUNDERBOLT AND SUICIDE.

Ruby read on. 'In Cape Town today, Mr Johnny Lance said, "This is good news for Van Der Byl Diamonds. This is going to be one of the richest underwater diamond fields[29] in the world. The company will begin dredging[30] before the end of the year . . . " '

Ruby looked at Benedict. His eyes were filling with tears.

'Lance! I hate him! I hate him! He beats me every time. Oh God, I hate him.'

Ruby could not understand.

'Aren't you pleased?' she asked. 'Van Der Byl Diamonds will make millions.'

'No, no,' Benedict cried. 'Listen . . .' and Benedict began to explain. Johnny Lance had always done better than him. Johnny had always succeeded when he, Benedict, had failed.

'Now do you understand?' Benedict said at last. 'And I wanted to beat him, to ruin him.'

Ruby was silent. Then, 'What are you going to do about it?' she said.

'But I've told you. There's nothing I can do. Johnny always wins.'

'Nonsense,' Ruby replied angrily. 'We can find a way to stop him, if we work together.'

Benedict looked up.

'Do you really think so?' he said. 'But how? If there are diamonds at Thunderbolt and Suicide, *Kingfisher* will get them up.'

'*Kingfisher*,' Ruby said. 'Tell me more about this ship, Benedict. Take me to see *Kingfisher*. Tell me how she works.'

Benedict was excited now.

'Of course, Ruby! We'll look at *Kingfisher* before she leaves England. Perhaps we can get the diamonds – not Johnny!'

5

Kingfisher in Las Palmas

Benedict van der Byl and Ruby Lance drove from London to see the ship, *Kingfisher,* before she sailed for South Africa. Benedict talked alone with Captain Sergio Caporetti.

When *Kingfisher* reached the island of Las Palmas, the captain sent a telegram to Johnny: PROBLEM WITH ENGINES. HAVE TO STOP IN LAS PALMAS FOR TEN DAYS.

Johnny was angry, but he could do nothing.

A Japanese computer expert[31] was waiting at Las Palmas. His name was Kaminikoto. Kaminikoto had had a long talk with Benedict in London.

Sergio showed Kaminikoto round *Kingfisher*.

'Yes, I see how it works,' said Kaminikoto. 'The gravel is dredged up from the sea-bed. Then the small bits of rock and mud are dried and carried along a conveyor belt[32] in a tunnel to the x-ray[33] room. The x-ray machine finds the diamonds in the gravel. The diamonds are taken out of the gravel and graded[34] by the computer. When the diamonds are graded they are put in a strong, closed compartment.

'Yes, it's clever,' Kaminikoto went on, 'the conveyor belt, the x-ray machine and the computer do everything.

'We will put in a second machine in the conveyor tunnel.

23

Our machine will find the best diamonds first and keep them. Only the smallest diamonds will be left for the Van Der Byl Company.'

'Will it be easy to fit in your machine?' Sergio asked.

'We will have to move the inspection hatch[35] back about three metres,' replied Kaminikoto. 'That's all. I don't think anyone will notice it.'

There was a party for the arrival of *Kingfisher* at Cartridge Bay. There were many guests at the party. Johnny had invited many important people. Some of them had lent money to Van Der Byl Diamonds. Everyone was eating and drinking.

Johnny saw Tracey and smiled at her. Ruby was there too. She was talking to Benedict. They had become good friends since Ruby's visit to London. Johnny was pleased. He was pleased with anything which made Ruby happy.

When *Kingfisher* arrived, Sergio Caporetti welcomed the guests.

Johnny took Mr Larsen round the ship himself. Larsen's Finance Company had loaned Johnny the money to build *Kingfisher*.

Johnny explained how everything worked. He told Larsen about the conveyor belts, the x-ray machine and the computer. Benedict and Ruby listened. When Johnny saw the new inspection hatch, he stopped for a moment and then moved on.

'He saw that it has been moved,' Benedict whispered to Ruby.

'Yes, but he didn't say anything,' she answered. 'When will you tell Johnny about us?'

'The diamonds *Kingfisher* finds at Thunderbolt and Suicide will be worthless,' said Benedict. 'Then the company will be ruined. And Johnny will be ruined too. That's when I'll tell him!'

Later, Benedict walked across to where Johnny and Larsen

Johnny explained how everything worked.

were standing on deck. Benedict smiled and said, 'Well, you've got your toy now, Johnny. I hope you can do something with it!'

'Toy, Mr van der Byl?' said Larsen. 'Why do you think *Kingfisher* is a toy? Don't you think Mr Lance will succeed?'

'Well, I'm not sure,' Benedict answered. 'But you are lending him all the money, not me. I hope Johnny is right. I hope *Kingfisher* will find diamonds.'

There was a silence. Then, 'Well, I hope so too,' Larsen said. 'Thank you, Mr van der Byl. Thank you, Mr Lance.' He walked away.

'And thank you, Benedict van der Byl,' Johnny said angrily, when the two men were alone. 'At the end of this week, you'll see that you are wrong. *Kingfisher* is not a toy.'

'We'll see,' Benedict said, smiling, and he walked away.

The guests were leaving now. Planes were taking them back to Cape Town.

After the guests had gone, everything was quiet. It was dark. The stars shone hard and bright, like diamonds. Johnny sat in the Land Rover, thinking. Something was worrying him. Something on *Kingfisher* had been changed. Then he shook his head and drove slowly down to where *Kingfisher* was waiting.

The ship's engines were running. Johnny went up onto the bridge where Sergio was with another man. This was Hugo Kramer, captain of *Wild Goose*. *Wild Goose* was going to bring supplies of food to *Kingfisher*. Benedict had made sure that this job was given to Kramer.

As soon as Kramer left the ship, *Kingfisher* set off for Thunderbolt and Suicide.

It was after midnight when Johnny went to his cabin. He lay down, but he was excited and could not sleep. He thought about Thunderbolt and Suicide. He and Tracey had gone diving there. They had walked on the sea-bed. Johnny had smelt the diamonds! He knew they were there. With the help of *Kingfisher*, he was going to get them up. At last, he fell asleep.

6

The Dredging Begins

As the sun came up, *Kingfisher* reached the white rocks of Thunderbolt and Suicide.

Wild Goose was there, waiting for them. It was not easy to anchor[36] *Kingfisher* in the right place. The sea near the islands was very rough.

By the afternoon, *Kingfisher* was ready. She was anchored over the place where Johnny hoped to find diamonds.

'I'll begin the dredging now,' Johnny said.

'Can I watch?' Sergio asked.

'All right, come down,' Johnny answered.

The two men went down to the computer room. Johnny unlocked the heavy door. He sat down and fed the program[37] into the computer.

'This is very clever, Johnny,' Sergio said. Johnny did not know that Sergio had worked with Kaminikoto in Las Palmas.

Johnny stood up. 'OK. Let's go up on deck,' he said.

The two men went up on deck and watched the heavy machinery start to move. The dredge head[38] on the end of a long, black hose went down through a square hole in the deck. The hose moved through the hole like a black snake. The dredge head moved slowly down to the sea-bed.

With a loud, roaring noise, the pumps began to work. Air was pulling up sea-water and gravel from the sea-bed. The sea-water and gravel came up the hose into *Kingfisher*.

The pumps roared for three days and three nights. The dredge head moved over every centimetre of the sea-bed between Thunderbolt and Suicide. On the evening of the third day, Johnny stopped the pumps. Johnny was beaten. He had failed. The diamonds they had found were small and poor.

*The dredge head on the end of a long, black hose went
down through a square hole in the deck.*

Van Der Byl Diamond Company was finished. Johnny Lance was a ruined man.

———

Early the following morning, Johnny Lance left *Kingfisher*.

Sergio watched from the bridge as Johnny went on board *Wild Goose*.

'Good luck, Johnny,' Sergio shouted. The Italian was sorry for Johnny. Sergio liked Johnny. But Sergio remembered the twenty-five thousand pounds Benedict had paid him.

The fat Italian walked down to the control room. He opened the door and locked it behind him. He took a piece of blue paper from his pocket. At the top of the paper were the words: KAMINIKOTO COMPUTER PROGRAM.

Ten minutes later, Sergio left the control room. He went to the conveyor room. After twenty minutes, he had removed the inspection hatch.

Sergio was a very fat man. He had to push hard to get through the small, square hole of the inspection hatch. At last, he was inside.

Sergio crawled along the conveyor tunnel until he came to Kaminikoto's machine. He put his hand down behind the computer and lifted out a metal cup. He shone a light into the cup and laughed quietly. The cup was full of diamonds. He poured the diamonds into a bag.

Sergio put the metal cup back behind the computer. He pushed himself back along the conveyor belt to the inspection hatch. Then he pushed himself out through the small, square hole.

Four hours later, Hugo Kramer returned with the *Wild Goose*. He went on board the *Kingfisher*.

'Has Johnny gone?' Sergio asked.

'Yes,' Hugo answered. 'He took the plane from Cartridge

Bay. He should be in Cape Town by now. Have you got the diamonds?'

'Yes, come and see,' Sergio said.

He took Hugo into his cabin and locked the door. He took the small bag from a drawer in his desk and poured out the diamonds.

There were hundreds of stones. But there, in the middle, was the biggest diamond Hugo and Sergio had ever seen.

It was beautiful. The two men knew that they were looking at one of the great diamonds of the world.

'We must tell Mr van der Byl immediately,' said Kramer. 'He'll know what to do.'

7

'I've Won, Johnny!'

When Benedict got Kramer's message, he went to Larsen. Larsen's Finance Company had loaned the money to build *Kingfisher*.

'Johnny Lance has failed,' Benedict told Larsen. 'The diamonds he has found are poor and small. Lance will not be able to pay back your money. But the company has my father's name. I will use my own money to save the company.'

'I understand,' said Larsen. 'I'll have the papers prepared at once.'

Twenty minutes later, Benedict signed the papers. He walked quickly to his car where Ruby was waiting.

'I've got it!' said Benedict with a laugh. He looked at his watch. 'I want you to go and wait in my office. I'm going to the Board Meeting[39] now. I'll phone you when I want you to come.'

'I'll be waiting,' Ruby said.

30

As the car stopped, Benedict said, 'This will be one of the best moments of my life.'

———

The Board Room was at the top of the building. The big windows looked out onto Table Mountain.

Johnny Lance was standing at one end of the table. He was thinner and he looked tired. There were some papers on the table in front of him, but he did not look at them.

'We dredged for sixty-six hours,' Johnny said. 'We found a few small diamonds, but they are worth only one thousand pounds. And we spent six and a half thousand pounds getting them out.'

Johnny stopped and looked round the table. Tracey's face was pale and she looked sadly at Johnny. Benedict was looking out of the window, with a smile on his face.

Benedict turned towards them.

'You have to pay the interest[40] on the loan at the end of the month – in three days' time. Where are you going to find one hundred and fifty thousand rand, Johnny?'

'Larsen will wait for a few weeks,' Johnny answered.

'But it is not Larsen's decision,' Benedict said quietly. 'I've paid back all the money to Larsen. You now owe me the money and I'm not going to wait. You have ruined my father's company, Lance. Now I want your shares[41].'

Benedict turned to Tracey.

'And I want your shares, too,' he said.

'No,' said Tracey.

'OK. Then I'll get everything from Johnny. I'll get the company and Johnny will be a ruined man.'

There was a long silence.

'I've got three days before I have to pay the interest,' Johnny said.

31

'You can have three days,' Benedict answered with a smile. 'But after three days, you are finished.'

Johnny picked up his papers and took his jacket from the back of his chair.

'Wait,' said Benedict.

'What for?' Johnny asked.

Benedict picked up a phone. 'Come in, please, darling,' he said.

As the door opened, Benedict walked towards Ruby Lance and kissed her on the mouth. The two of them looked at Johnny.

'The company is not the only thing I've taken from you,' Benedict said, smiling at Johnny.

'I want a divorce,' said Ruby. 'Benedict and I are going to be married.'

Johnny looked at them. He took a step towards Benedict.

'No, Johnny, don't hit him,' said Tracey. 'That's what he wants you to do!'

'I've won, Johnny. I've won!' Benedict laughed.

Johnny looked at Ruby. 'The house is yours, Ruby,' he said quietly. 'I won't go there again. I'll stay in a hotel. You can send my clothes to the hotel.'

———

Johnny went to a hotel. He went into his room and lay on the bed and closed his eyes. He did not know what to do. He could not sleep. He poured some whisky into a glass and drank it quickly. Then he had another drink and another.

As Johnny lay there, he heard a knock on the door. He got up and opened it. Tracey came into the room.

He took her in his arms and she kissed him. They held each other tightly.

———

In Tracey's arms, Johnny felt strong again. He was not beaten. He was going to fight.

'We've still got three days,' he said. 'I'll find those diamonds. I know they are there.'

Johnny looked at his watch.

'It's four o'clock. I'll take the company plane. I can get to Cartridge Bay just after dark. Send a radio message to Cartridge Bay. Tell them I'm coming. *Wild Goose* must be ready to take me out to *Kingfisher* . . .'

'I'll do it now,' Tracey said. 'Hurry. I'll be here, waiting for you when you come back.'

8

'I'll Tell You Everything'

Benedict and Ruby were in the Old Man's study. Benedict was angry – very, very angry. He walked up and down. Ruby watched him. She knew now that Benedict would never be a happy man.

'Benedict,' she said, 'I'm going home now. I'm going to send Johnny's clothes to his hotel. Then you and I will be together forever.'

She tried to kiss Benedict, but he turned his face away.

'Don't do that,' he said. 'I tried to beat him, but he wasn't beaten. I was watching Johnny's face. He was pleased to hear that you were leaving him.

'I wanted to take you from Johnny Lance, but he didn't want to keep you. If Lance doesn't want you, then I don't want you either. Why don't you go? Leave me alone. I don't want you.'

'Benedict,' Ruby whispered. 'That's not true, is it? You don't want me to go, do you?'

33

'Yes, I do,' said Benedict angrily. 'You've been paid enough, haven't you? You've got a fur coat, diamonds . . . it's finished now. Why don't you go home and leave me alone?'

'Have you forgotten about the computer?' Ruby said slowly. 'I know about the computer in *Kingfisher* . . .'

As soon as Ruby said this, she knew she had made a mistake.

'If you tell anyone,' Benedict whispered, 'I'll kill you. You know I will. You've been paid. Now get out!'

'All right,' she said. 'I'll go.'

———

Ruby drove slowly. Her eyes were full of tears.

'I hate Benedict,' she whispered. 'I hate him.'

Ruby drove on. As she drove, she began to make plans. She now knew what she was going to do.

Ruby drove towards Johnny's hotel. She drove faster. She knew what she was going to say to Johnny.

Ruby stopped the car and ran into the hotel.

'I must see Mr Lance,' she told the girl at the desk.

'I'm sorry, madam. Mr Lance left an hour ago,' the girl answered.

At that moment, Tracey walked out of the lift.

'Where is Johnny?' Ruby asked. 'Where has he gone? I must see him.'

'Johnny's flown to Cartridge Bay,' Tracey said.

'Then you must follow him. Charter[42] a plane,' Ruby said.

'They won't land at Cartridge Bay after dark,' Tracey told her.

'Then you must follow him by car,' said Ruby. 'You can get there in eight hours.'

'But why?' Tracey asked. 'What's happened?'

'I'll tell you why. I'll tell you everything,' Ruby answered. 'Sergio Caporetti and Hugo Kramer are working for Benedict.

You've got to get to Cartridge Bay and tell Johnny. Tell him before it's too late!'

———

Johnny looked at his watch. In another half-hour he would be at Cartridge Bay.

A strong wind was blowing. Below him, a thick cloud of dust was blowing across the desert. Johnny could not see through the dust. He had to fly lower.

A message came over the radio. A storm was coming. He was told to go back.

I can't go back now, Johnny said to himself.

He switched off the radio and flew on.

Suddenly he saw the bright lights of the landing strip[43] at Cartridge Bay. Johnny brought the plane down fast. He had reached Cartridge Bay. Now he had to get to *Kingfisher* and find diamonds!

———

Far away from Cartridge Bay, Tracey was driving the big car through a thick cloud of dust. She was not on a road now, but on a rough track. But Tracey drove faster. She had to tell Johnny! They were all Johnny's enemies – Sergio, Kramer and Benedict.

Tracey drove all night. She reached Cartridge Bay just before the sun came up. Johnny must be on *Kingfisher* by now. She had to be careful. Johnny's enemies were everywhere.

Tracey saw Kramer on the deck of *Wild Goose*.

'Did you take Lance out to *Kingfisher*?' Tracey asked.

'Yes,' Kramer said, looking at Tracey in surprise, 'I got back here a few minutes ago.'

'You fool!' Tracey shouted. 'He knows everything. We'll all go to prison. I've got to stop him. Take me out to *Kingfisher* at once!'

'But where's Benedict van der Byl? Why didn't he come himself?' Kramer asked.

'Lance had a fight with Benedict. He's in hospital, so I had to come. Quick. Get me out to *Kingfisher* now.'

'I can get you out there but I won't be able to wait. I can't stay out there in this storm. *Wild Goose* is too small. And you will be alone. What can you do?'

'Don't worry. The Italian will help me,' Tracey said.

'But I didn't know you were in the plan,' said Kramer.

'Benedict and I would never let a stranger take our diamonds!' Tracey said, laughing.

Hugo Kramer smiled.

'Come on,' he said. 'Let's go.'

9

In the Old Man's Study

Benedict van der Byl sat alone in his father's study. He was thinking about the Old Man.

Why had his father brought Johnny Lance into the family? Johnny Lance had beaten him in everything – in sport, in business, in love. Now he had beaten Johnny in business. But Johnny had given Ruby to him. Johnny had not wanted her.

Benedict looked round the study. This was where the Old Man had killed himself. Benedict looked at the guns in the cupboard. He stood up and went to the cupboard. He took out a gun and held it against his head. He pulled the trigger[44].

'Click, click!' Benedict laughed. He knew the gun was empty.

Benedict took some cartridges and loaded the gun. He held it against his head for a moment. Then he laughed and put the gun down on his father's desk.

Benedict poured himself a glass of brandy. He was frightened and excited. He sat staring at the cold, powerful gun.

Four hours late, Benedict was still sitting in the Old Man's study. His handsome face was red. He was drunk. The gun was still on the desk.

The door opened.

'So you've come back,' he said.

Ruby walked into the room. She was wearing the beautiful fur coat that Benedict had given her. Her golden hair was shining brightly.

Ruby saw the gun on the desk. She was afraid. But she spoke in a strong voice.

'Yes, I've come back,' she said. 'I've come back to tell you something.

'Tracey is on her way to Cartridge Bay,' Ruby went on. 'I told her everything. In a few hours, Johnny will know about the computer, the large diamond, everything. You've lost again, my darling. Johnny's beaten you again.'

Benedict shouted madly. He jumped towards her. His hands went round her throat. Ruby screamed.

They fought together and then they fell onto the floor. Benedict hit his head on the desk. Ruby jumped up and ran towards the door. Benedict stood up and took the gun from the desk.

Benedict fired. Ruby turned and fell onto the floor.

Benedict fired again – into Ruby's beautiful face.

Benedict van der Byl looked down at the woman he had killed.

Benedict fired.

He shook with fear. The metal of the gun was cold in his hands.

No, no, Benedict whispered to himself. I didn't do it, I didn't do it!

He walked out of the house to the garage. He threw the gun and a box of cartridges onto the back seat of the car. He sat down behind the wheel. He must get away! But how? Where to?

Yes! He must get to *Wild Goose*. Kramer could take him across the sea – perhaps to South America. He would be safe there. And he had money – lots of money – in a bank in Switzerland.

Benedict drove the car out of the garage and started on the long journey to Cartridge Bay.

10

On Kingfisher

Johnny and Sergio Caporetti stood together on the bridge of *Kingfisher*.

The ship was in the middle of the storm. The roaring wind was blowing all around them. The waves were crashing against the white rocks of Thunderbolt and Suicide.

Twice during the night, Johnny had moved *Kingfisher*. Each time, *Kingfisher* had moved nearer the sharp rocks. Twice, the dredge head had gone down and moved over the sea-bed. Twice, Johnny had gone down to the control room and studied the computer reports. But only a few small, poor diamonds had been found. Johnny Lance moved *Kingfisher* again. Nearer and nearer the rocks. Sergio was worried.

'Don't worry, Sergio,' Johnny told him. 'The computer knows where we are. Nothing will happen to *Kingfisher*.'

'But the computer can't see those sharp rocks!' said Sergio. 'I can!'

'I'm going down to the control room again,' Johnny told him.

Johnny studied the computer reports again. No diamonds had been found. He knew there were diamonds there – in the gap between Thunderbolt and Suicide. But they had found nothing.

Suddenly Johnny was wild with anger. He picked up the computer reports and threw them onto the floor. But then he saw a piece of blue paper lying on the table.

What was it? Johnny picked up the paper and looked at it. At the top of the paper were the words: KAMINIKOTO COMPUTER PROGRAM.

Johnny looked carefully. It was a computer program. What was it doing there? He would ask Sergio.

Johnny ran back to the bridge. But before he could say anything, Sergio called out, 'Look, it's *Wild Goose*. What's she doing here?'

Johnny pushed the piece of blue paper into his pocket. He looked down at *Wild Goose*. The waves were crashing over the small boat. Suddenly he saw Tracey. She was going to jump from the *Wild Goose* to the ladder on the side of *Kingfisher*!

'No!' Johnny shouted. 'Don't jump! Go back!' But Tracey jumped and caught the ladder with one hand. Her legs were in the water. She was going to fall!

Johnny ran down the ladder and pulled her up onto the deck of *Kingfisher*.

'What does she want?' Sergio asked. 'She nearly killed herself when she jumped.'

'I don't know, but I'm going to find out,' Johnny told him. 'You stay up here and keep the ship off those rocks.'

Johnny took Tracey down to his cabin. Tracey told Johnny

everything. She spoke so quickly that, at first, he could not understand her.

'You must stop them, Johnny!' Tracey said. 'You must stop them. The diamonds are yours.'

Then Johnny remembered the piece of blue paper he had found in the control room.

'Come with me,' he said.

He took Tracey into the control room and locked the heavy door behind them.

Tracey watched as Johnny fed the new program into the computer. They stared at the screen.

On the screen, they saw lists of all the diamonds that had been found. They were rich! The company was saved.

'So I was right,' Johnny said at last. 'But where have they put the diamonds? They must be somewhere on the ship.'

But then he remembered.

'They moved the inspection hatch!' Johnny said. 'I knew something on *Kingfisher* had been changed. So the diamonds are in the conveyor tunnel. Come on!'

———

Sergio Caporetti was worried. Why had Tracey come out to *Kingfisher*? What were Johnny and Tracey talking about?

The big Italian ran down to his cabin. He unlocked his desk and took out the bag of diamonds. Sergio put the bag into his jacket pocket. As he went back to the bridge, Sergio saw that the control room door was open. He looked at the computer screen. All the diamonds were listed on the screen.

'Johnny's found the program!' Sergio whispered. 'What can I do?'

He looked at the long handle on the cabin door. It was heavy and made of metal. He took it off the door and held it in his hand behind his back.

Where were Johnny and Tracey? As quietly as possible, Sergio went down to the conveyor room. The big Italian looked carefully through the open door.

The cover was off the inspection hatch. Johnny was getting into the tunnel. He shouted down to Tracey, 'Get me a spanner from the tool cupboard.'

When Tracey went to the cupboard, Sergio came up behind her. He raised the heavy metal handle. Then he stopped. No, he could not kill a girl. Tracey ran back to Johnny with the spanner.

Tracey climbed into the conveyor tunnel. She held the light while Johnny looked around. He put his hand behind Kaminikoto's machine.

'There's something here,' said Johnny. 'It's a metal cup.'

Johnny lifted out the metal cup. It was full of diamonds. Johnny and Tracey laughed with happiness and excitement.

'Come on,' Johnny said. 'Let's get out of here. We'll lock Sergio and the crew in a cabin. I'll sail *Kingfisher* back to Cartridge Bay. Then we'll find the others – and your brother too!'

They climbed out of the tunnel and Johnny ran towards the door.

He pushed at the heavy door, but it would not open. He tried to open the door to the cyclone room[45]. It was locked too! There was no way out. Johnny looked through the thick glass of the small window. The cyclone room was empty.

Johnny went back to Tracey and put his arm round her shoulders.

'We've got problems,' he said. 'Sergio knows. He's locked us in.'

The big Italian looked carefully through the open door.

11

'We've Got to Get Away!'

W*ild Goose* got back to Cartridge Bay after a long, hard journey. As the boat moved closer to land, Kramer saw someone waiting for him. It was a man – holding a gun. Who was it?

'My God, it's Benedict,' said Kramer. Suddenly, he felt very afraid.

Benedict van der Byl jumped onto the deck of *Wild Goose*. He looked around angrily.

'Where have you been? What's happened?' he shouted.

'I thought you were in hospital!' Kramer said.

'Who told you that?'

'Your sister.'

'Tracey? You've seen her? Where is she?' Benedict shouted.

'I took her out to *Kingfisher*,' Kramer replied. 'She said Johnny knew everything. She's going to stop him getting the diamonds.'

'You fool!' Benedict shouted. 'She won't stop him. She'll help him. She's in love with him!'

Benedict thought for a moment, then he said, 'Have you got food and water on *Wild Goose*?'

'Yes, enough for three, perhaps four weeks,' Kramer answered quickly.

'Good,' said Benedict. 'We've got to get away.'

'Get away? Where to?'

'South America.'

Kramer looked at Benedict carefully. Benedict's eyes were red and he was covered with dust and dirt.

'What about money?' Kramer asked slowly, looking at the gun Benedict was holding.

'I've got money,' Benedict answered.

44

'How much? How much for me?' Kramer asked.

'Ten thousand pounds.'

Kramer shook his head.

'Twenty,' Benedict said quickly. Ruby's body was in his father's study. Perhaps the police had found it already.

'Fifty. I want fifty,' Kramer said. 'You need me – you need *Wild Goose* – you know that.'

'OK. Fifty,' said Benedict, thinking again of Ruby's body.

———

Wild Goose left the land behind. The wind roared all around them. The waves crashed against the sides of the little boat.

'Turn on the radio,' said Benedict.

'The radio? In this storm?' Kramer laughed. 'You won't hear anything.'

But Benedict moved across to the radio and turned it on. They heard a voice.

'Calling *Wild Goose*! Calling *Wild Goose*. This is *Kingfisher* calling *Wild Goose*. Come in, *Wild Goose*.'

'Don't answer,' shouted Kramer. 'It's a trick!' But Benedict answered.

'Hello, *Kingfisher*. This is *Wild Goose*.'

The answer was loud and clear.

'This is Captain Caporetti. Who's that?'

'Benedict van der Byl.'

'There's been some trouble here,' said Caporetti. 'But it's finished now. I'm in charge[46]. I've got some "guests." But I've locked them up.'

'We must get to *Kingfisher*,' said Kramer. 'We must pick up Caporetti and the diamonds.'

'I have to get onto *Kingfisher*,' said Benedict. 'I've got to remove Kaminikoto's computer program. It's got his name on it. The police will find him and then they will find us.'

Benedict spoke into the radio again.
'*Kingfisher*. We're coming now. And I'm coming aboard.'
'OK. I'll be waiting for you,' the Italian answered.

———

Two hours later, *Wild Goose* had reached *Kingfisher*. The storm
was still blowing. The wind blew *Wild Goose* near to the side
of *Kingfisher*. Benedict jumped across the gap and caught
Kingfisher's ladder. He climbed up quickly onto the deck.

'Where is Lance?' Benedict asked Sergio.

Sergio Caporetti took him into his cabin and shut the door.

'Lance and your sister are locked in the conveyor room. They
found out about the Japanese program. But there's nothing they
can do about it.'

'Good,' Benedict said. He had a plan now.

'Listen, Caporetti,' he went on. 'We've got to remove that
program from the computer. Then *Wild Goose* will take us and the
diamonds to South America. Give them to me now.'

Sergio smiled and touched his jacket pocket.

'No, I think I'll keep them,' he said.

'OK,' said Benedict. 'Go down to the computer room and
remove the program from the computer.'

Caporetti did not move.

'What about my crew?' he said. 'They're good men. I don't
want any trouble for them.'

'I'll talk to them,' Benedict said. 'Call them up here and then
start removing that program.'

When the five crewmen were standing in front of him,
Benedict said, 'Get ready to leave the ship. I'm now in charge.
Go down to your cabins and get your things.'

The crewmen were surprised. But they went down towards
their cabins. Benedict walked behind them, his gun in his hand.

46

'Stop!' Benedict shouted. He pointed to a door on the right. 'Open that door and get inside!' he said. The men saw the gun. They went inside. Benedict shut the heavy door and locked it.

Benedict moved quickly. He stopped outside a door with the words: "Explosives. No Entry" written on it.

•Benedict got out some keys and opened the door. Inside, he picked up some plastic explosive[47] and some time-fuses. He put the time-fuses in his pocket and the plastic explosive round his neck. Then he went quickly to the cyclone room.

He put his gun down near the door. He put the plastic explosive round the cyclone and pushed the time-fuses into it.

In the conveyor room, on the other side of the small window, Johnny saw what Benedict was doing.

'Look,' he said to Tracey.

'Benedict!' she cried. 'What's he doing?'

'He's putting plastic explosive in the cyclone room,' said Johnny. 'When it explodes, gravel and water will pour into the room. *Kingfisher* will sink and we will be drowned.'

'No!' cried Tracey. 'He's my brother. He's not that bad. He won't murder us.'

'That's what he is going to do,' Johnny said.

Tracey looked through the small window again.

'No, Benedict,' she whispered. 'Please don't do it!'

Benedict turned and saw the two faces at the window. He stared and then smiled. Then he turned and left the room.

'He'll come back,' Tracey said. 'He won't do it.'

'I think he will,' Johnny answered quietly.

'No, Benedict,' she whispered. 'Please don't do it!'

12

'You've Killed Them All!'

Benedict went back up on deck. *Wild Goose* was coming nearer to *Kingfisher*. The sea was crashing against the side of the ships. Where was Caporetti? He had the diamonds. Benedict could not leave without him.

At that moment, Sergio Caporetti came down from the bridge.

'Come on! Hurry up!' Benedict called.

'Where are my crew?' Caporetti shouted.

'They're all right,' Benedict answered. 'I sent them to . . .'

At that moment, there was a loud explosion on *Kingfisher*.

'You've killed them all!' shouted Caporetti. 'My crew, Johnny, the girl . . .'

Benedict pointed the gun at the Italian captain.

'Stay where you are,' he said. 'Stay where you are or I'll shoot you. Give me the diamonds. Give me the diamonds and you can come with us.'

'OK,' Caporetti answered. He put his hand into his jacket. He took out the heavy bag of diamonds and swung it hard at Benedict's face.

But Benedict was ready for him. He turned and lifted the gun. It hit the Italian's hand and the bag of diamonds fell onto the deck.

At that moment, a big wave crashed over the deck and Caporetti shouted, 'Look out! The bag! It's going to go into the sea!' Benedict jumped and caught the bag. Caporetti ran along the deck towards the bridge.

Benedict pushed the bag of diamonds into his pocket and pointed the gun.

'Stop or I'll shoot!' he shouted. But the Italian did not stop. Benedict fired the gun.

The shot hit Caporetti in the back, but he ran on. Benedict fired again, but it was too late. Caporetti was on the bridge.

Wild Goose was now beside *Kingfisher*.

'Have you gone mad?' Kramer shouted at Benedict. 'We'll all be hanged[48]. We've got to go – now!'

'Wait!' Benedict shouted. 'Wait! I'm coming.'

He climbed quickly down the ladder and jumped onto the deck of *Wild Goose*. As he landed, the gun fell from his hand into the sea.

'What have you done, you fool?' Kramer shouted. 'That explosion will sink *Kingfisher*. And why were you shooting at the Italian?'

'He had the diamonds,' said Benedict.

'Haven't you got the diamonds?' Kramer shouted.

'I tried to get them . . .' Benedict said.

Kramer hit Benedict on the face. Benedict kicked Kramer hard and he shouted with pain.

'I'm in charge, Kramer,' Benedict said quietly. 'Take me to South America and you will have fifty thousand pounds. Without me, you get nothing.'

At that moment, there was a loud crash.

Kramer ran to the bridge but he was too late. *Wild Goose* had hit one of *Kingfisher's* anchor cables. The thick, steel cable went round and round *Wild Goose's* propeller[49]. The propeller broke off and sank to the bottom of the sea.

Kramer could do nothing. In front of them were the sharp, white rocks of Thunderbolt and Suicide. Kramer could not control *Wild Goose*. The boat was going to crash on the rocks.

———

Johnny was holding Tracey in his arms.

Suddenly, there was a loud explosion. The blast hurt her ears. Tracey and Johnny were thrown across the room. But they were still alive!

Johnny stood up and looked into the cyclone room. Mud, gravel and sea water were pouring into the cyclone room.

In a few minutes, water, gravel and mud had come up past the small window. The steel sides of the room began to break. Water and mud were pouring into the conveyor room. Tracey and Johnny were trapped.

Tracey and Johnny were pushed against the wall. The water and mud came up over their knees. Then up past their waists.

Tracey began to scream and scream. Johnny held her tightly in his arms. This was the end.

Suddenly, the door behind him opened. Johnny fell back, still holding Tracey. Sergio Caporetti was in the doorway. He took Tracey into his arms.

Slowly, Caporetti climbed up to the deck, still holding Tracey. Johnny saw blood all over the Italian's back. Caporetti turned to Johnny.

'Get to the control room, quick!' he said. 'Stop the dredging or *Kingfisher* will sink!'

Johnny pushed his way to the control room. He turned off the controls, one by one. The dredging stopped. And there was silence. *Kingfisher* moved from side to side in the wild waves.

Feeling sick and weak, Johnny climbed slowly up onto the bridge.

Less than two hundred metres away, he saw the white, sharp rocks of Thunderbolt and Suicide. The wild waves were crashing onto the rocks. Johnny watched in horror as *Kingfisher* moved nearer and nearer to the terrible rocks. Then he heard Sergio say quietly, 'I can't turn *Kingfisher*. We'll have to go through the gap.'

'No!' Johnny cried. 'It's not possible!'

But *Kingfisher* was moving nearer to that terrible gap. Suddenly, Johnny shouted, 'My God! It's *Wild Goose*!'

51

Suddenly, the door behind him opened.

Sergio looked at *Wild Goose* and laughed.

'Benedict van der Byl, you tried to kill me and my crew,' he shouted. 'Now I'm going to kill you!'

'Sergio! You can't do it! It's murder!' Johnny shouted.

The men on *Wild Goose* saw *Kingfisher* coming towards them. They jumped into the sea. Benedict van der Byl was holding the side of a rubber raft[50] with both hands.

And then – nothing! *Wild Goose* had gone. The boat had sunk beneath the sea. A huge wave carried *Kingfisher* through the gap between Thunderbolt and Suicide. The ship was through and into the open sea.

13

At the Red Gods

After midnight, the wind stopped blowing. The storm was over. Stars shone like diamonds in the black sky.

'You've been badly hurt,' Johnny said to Sergio. 'You must rest now. Tracey will look at your back.'

'No,' Sergio answered. 'This is my ship. I'm sailing her to Cartridge Bay. You call Cartridge Bay on the radio. Tell them we're coming.'

Johnny spoke to Cartridge Bay on the radio. He told them what had happened. He asked for a doctor.

'And we'll want the police, too,' he said.

'The police are here already, Mr Lance. They are looking for Mr Benedict van der Byl. They'd like to speak to you now.'

'Sorry, no,' Johnny answered. 'I'll talk later. Make sure that a doctor is there when we arrive.'

'Why did you help us, Sergio?' Johnny asked the Italian quietly.

'Johnny, I've done bad things in my life,' Sergio answered. 'But when I heard the explosion, I knew I had to get you both out.'

'The Japanese computer program found a lot of diamonds,' said Johnny. 'I saw them listed on the computer screen. What happened to them?'

'Benedict put them in his jacket pocket,' replied Sergio. 'Now they're at the bottom of the sea.

'And there was one large, beautiful diamond,' Sergio went on. 'It was the biggest, most beautiful diamond I have ever seen. It's now lost forever.'

Kingfisher reached Cartridge Bay just before midday. Sergio had lost a lot of blood and was very weak. But he sailed the ship all the way. The doctor and the police came onto the ship at once.

First, the police told Johnny about Ruby's death. So Benedict is a murderer, he thought. Then the police questioned Johnny for two hours.

'Two last questions,' the policeman said to Johnny. 'Was the crash between *Wild Goose* and *Kingfisher* an accident?'

'Yes, an accident,' Johnny answered.

'And do you think anyone from *Wild Goose* is alive?'

'No,' Johnny said.

When the policeman had left, Johnny went to speak to the doctor.

'How is Caporetti?' Johnny asked him.

'He is very ill. I think he will die,' the doctor said.

Johnny went into Sergio's cabin.

'Sergio – your crew are all safe,' Johnny told him.

Sergio smiled. Then, suddenly, he could not breathe. He coughed and blood poured from his mouth. He fell back onto the bed and died.

The doctor gave Tracey some pills to make her sleep. But Johnny did not take any pills. He lay on the bed, thinking. He thought about Benedict, about *Kingfisher* and about the big diamond. Sergio had said, '. . . Benedict put the diamonds in his jacket pocket . . .'

Johnny got up and dressed quickly. He went and looked at a map. Forty eight kilometres north of Cartridge Bay was a place called the Red Gods.

The Red Gods were a line of red rocks rising from the sea. Johnny looked at the map carefully. Yes. The currents[51] from Thunderbolt and Suicide flowed towards the Red Gods. If someone fell into the sea at Thunderbolt and Suicide, the currents would throw them up onto the red rocks. Benedict's body would be there – with his jacket and the diamonds.

Johnny picked up the keys to the Land Rover and hurried to the garage. He opened the wide doors and checked the Land Rover carefully. The petrol tank was full. There was plenty of drinking water and a first-aid kit[52]. . . Yes, everything was there.

Johnny drove the Land Rover as fast as he could along the flat sand. As the sun came up, Johnny saw a hyena[53] run in front of the car.

The sun shone on the red rocks of the Red Gods. As he drove towards them, Johnny looked along the sand. There were hundreds of sea birds flying above the rocks.

The birds flew away as Johnny drove up. There was a body lying on the rocks. It was Hugo Kramer.

Then he saw the raft from *Wild Goose*. Johnny got out and walked slowly up to the raft. There were footprints in the sand beside the raft. Benedict was alive!

'Thank God,' Johnny whispered. 'Benedict's alive. Now I can kill him myself!'

There were footprints in the sand beside the raft.

14

'Don't Leave Me!'

Benedict's footprints went away from the raft, across the sand and into the desert.

There was a radio in the Land Rover. If Johnny called Cartridge Bay, the police helicopter would find Benedict in an hour.

No. Johnny decided not to tell the police. They thought that Benedict was dead. I can kill Benedict myself, he thought.

Johnny took his knife and cut the raft. All the air came out. Johnny threw it in the back of the Land Rover. Later, he would hide it in the desert. No one must know that Benedict had escaped from the sea.

Johnny drove into the desert, following Benedict's footprints. He saw a water-bottle lying on the ground. Benedict had thrown it away. Why? No one could live in this desert without water.

Johnny got out of the Land Rover and picked up the water bottle. The bottle was empty. Benedict was finished now!

Johnny looked at the footprints carefully. Benedict had run a little way and then sat down. Then the footprints went round in a circle and then on again towards the mountains.

Later, Benedict had fallen and lost a shoe. Johnny drove on carefully over the rocky ground. Then he saw something lying on the ground. It was Benedict's jacket.

Johnny remembered Caporetti's words, 'He put the diamonds in his jacket pocket.'

Johnny drove on faster. The Land Rover hit a sharp rock and stopped. Johnny jumped out and ran to the jacket. Yes, the bag was still there. Johnny took the bag back to the Land Rover and cut it open with his knife. The diamonds poured out and yes, there was the largest diamond he had ever seen!

Johnny held the beautiful diamond in his hands. He had worked all his life to find a diamond like this. He sat down beside the Land Rover and looked and looked at the beautiful stone.

Then Johnny smelt oil. He looked down at the ground under the Land Rover. Oil was pouring into the sand.

Johnny had not slept for two days. He was very, very tired. He closed his eyes.

When Johnny opened his eyes again he felt better. He looked at his watch. It was four o'clock in the afternoon. He ate some food and drank some water. Then he hid the bag of diamonds in the sand under the Land Rover.

He put some food, a water-bottle and the first-aid kit into a bag. He started to walk. He knew he would find Benedict soon. The footprints went from side to side and Benedict had fallen many times.

Johnny stopped. There were other prints now, animal prints. 'Hyenas!' Johnny whispered. 'Two of them.'

Benedict had cut himself on the sharp rocks. The hyenas had smelt blood. They would never leave him now. Then Johnny heard a terrible sound. It was the cry of the hyenas. It came from the other side of a sandy hill.

Johnny ran to the top of the hill and looked down. Benedict was lying on his back. His clothes were torn. One foot was covered with blood. A hyena sat three metres away. The other hyena was standing over Benedict's bleeding body. Johnny shouted and the animals ran away.

Johnny looked at Benedict. He knew he could not kill him now.

The sun was beginning to go down. They had to get back to the Land Rover and radio the police.

Johnny looked up. One of the hyenas had come back. It was waiting quietly for darkness.

Johnny sat beside Benedict until the moon came up. Then he stood up and lifted Benedict over his shoulders.

Benedict was very heavy. Johnny counted every step he took.

After two thousand, I'll rest, he thought. As he walked, the blood from Benedict's body fell onto Johnny's legs. The two hyenas followed. They could smell the blood.

Johnny rested, went on and rested again. Each time they rested, they drank some of the water. By one o'clock, all the water had gone. By two o'clock, Johnny knew they were lost.

Johnny fell down on the sand for the last time at five o'clock. Benedict lay beside him.

In an hour, the sun would be up. The heat of the sun would kill them both. That would be the end. Then the hyenas would eat them both. Johnny closed his eyes. There was nothing more he could do.

Later, Johnny heard a soft sound. He opened his eyes. A hyena was three metres away, watching them.

Johnny looked down at Benedict. Slowly, Benedict turned towards him.

'Who's there?' he whispered.

'Johnny.'

'Johnny?' said Benedict. 'I don't believe it. Give me some water.'

'The water's all gone,' Johnny said. He pointed to the two hyenas. 'Look!' he said. 'Now, I'm going and I'm leaving you here.'

Benedict gave a cry.

'No, Johnny. Please, Johnny. Johnny, don't leave me!' Benedict cried out.

Johnny got up. He walked a few steps away from Benedict. Then he stopped. He turned round and sat down on the sand. He could not leave Benedict to be killed by the hyenas.

The sun was burning Johnny's face. Both men lay without moving. The hyenas moved nearer and nearer.

Johnny suddenly remembered the smoke flares[54]. Slowly and carefully Johnny took a smoke flare from his bag. He lit a match and held the flame to the flare. He threw the flare towards the hyenas. Red smoke poured out of the flare and the animals ran away.

The red smoke blew over the two men. The smoke got into Johnny's eyes and mouth. He heard a roaring sound in his ears. A wind blew away the red smoke.

Johnny looked up. Twelve metres above him was a police helicopter. Johnny saw Tracey looking down at him. He saw her lips move.

'Johnny . . . I love you.'

'Johnny . . . I love you.'

POINTS
FOR
UNDERSTANDING

Points For Understanding

1

1 'Then how long have I got?' Jacobus van der Byl asked the doctor. What was the doctor's reply?

2 Why did Jacobus van der Byl want to see his lawyer?

3 What did Jacobus do after the lawyer had left?

4 Why was the Van Der Byl Diamond Company in trouble?

5 In his last will, Jacobus van der Byl made three people directors of the Van Der Byl Diamond Company. Who were the three people?

6 Who was pleased when Johnny Lance was made a director? Who was not pleased?

7 'There is something else,' the lawyer went on. What else was written in the will? What did it mean to Johnny Lance?

8 Benedict and Tracey were brother and sister. Was Johnny Lance related to them?

9 Why did Benedict hate Johnny?

10 'I will find more diamonds,' Johnny said.
   (a) Where was Johnny going to look for diamonds?
   (b) What was *Kingfisher*?
   (c) Who had designed the equipment on *Kingfisher*?

11 Why did Benedict laugh when Johnny spoke about *Kingfisher*?

12 Why was Benedict going to London?

13 Where was Johnny going to?

2

1 How was Johnny going to save the company?

2 Who was the captain of *Kingfisher*? Was he good at his job?

3 Johnny flew the plane low over Thunderbolt and Suicide.
   (a) What were Thunderbolt and Suicide?
   (b) Where was Johnny sure there were diamonds?
   (c) Why could the Van Der Byl Diamond Company not look for diamonds there?

4 Why was Hugo Kramer afraid of police patrols?

5 Hugo Kramer was waiting for the sun to go down. What was going to happen when it was dark?

6   Explain how the security officer sent the stolen diamonds to
    Hugo Kramer on the *Wild Goose*.
7   Explain how Hugo Kramer hid the stolen diamonds.
8   Where were the diamonds going to?

3

1   What was the bad mistake that Johnny had made?
2   What had happened to Tracey's marriage?
3   Why was Sergio Caporetti going to fly to London? Who was
    going with him?
4   Tracey threw some papers down on the table.
        (a) Who had owned the concession for Thunderbolt and Suicide?
        (b) Why had the government not taken the concession?
        (c) What had Tracey done?
5   Why did Benedict van der Byl smile when he saw the picture on
    the can of pilchards?
6   Benedict walked through a long room where some young men
    were cutting diamonds.
        (a) How do we know Benedict had been there before?
        (b) What was Benedict doing there?
        (c) Why was Benedict not going to make many more visits?
7   Benedict . . . watched the beautiful blonde coming towards him.
        (a) Who was the beautiful blonde?
        (b) Why was Benedict going to marry her?

4

1   Why did Ruby want Benedict to marry her?
2   Why did Ruby have to be careful?
3   What promise did Benedict ask Ruby to make?
4   Benedict led Ruby into the bedroom. What was lying on the bed?
5   What did Benedict buy Ruby in the old building in Soho?
6   As soon as Benedict saw the front page of the *Cape Argus*, his
    face changed.
        (a) What was the news on the front page?
        (b) Why was Benedict not pleased with the news?
7   Why were Benedict and Ruby going to look at *Kingfisher*?

5

1 Who did Benedict have a talk with on board *Kingfisher*?
2 Sergio Caporetti sent a telegram to Johnny.
    (a) Why did Caporetti say the *Kingfisher* had to stop at Las Palmas?
    (b) Who was Kaminikoto?
3 Explain how the machinery on *Kingfisher* worked.
4 Kaminikoto put a second machine on board *Kingfisher*.
    (a) What did Kaminikoto have to change in order to put in his machine?
    (b) What would his machine do?
5 Who was Mr Larsen?
6 What did Johnny do when he saw the new inspection hatch?
7 'When will you tell Johnny about us?' asked Ruby. What was Benedict's reply?
8 'Why do you think *Kingfisher* is a toy?' Mr Larsen asked Benedict.
    (a) Why had Benedict called *Kingfisher* a toy?
    (b) Why was Benedict sure that *Kingfisher* would not find any large diamonds?
9 Johnny sat in the Land Rover thinking.
    (a) Why was Johnny worried?
    (b) Why did he not do anything?
10 Hugo Kramer the captain of *Wild Goose*, was on board *Kingfisher*.
    (a) How was *Wild Goose* going to help *Kingfisher*?
    (b) Who had made sure that Kramer was given this job?
11 Why was Johnny sure that there were diamonds on the sea-bed between Thunderbolt and Suicide?

6

1 The two men went down to the computer room.
    (a) What did Johnny feed into the computer?
    (b) What was it Johnny did not know about Sergio?
2 Describe the start of the dredging.
3 Why was Johnny Lance a ruined man?
4 How much had Benedict paid Sergio Caporetti?
5 What was written on the piece of blue paper Sergio took from his pocket?
6 Why did Sergio find it hard to get through the inspection hatch?

7   Sergio crawled along the conveyor tunnel.
    (a) When did he stop?
    (b) Where did he put his hand?
    (c) What did he find?
8   Who came on board *Kingfisher*?
9   Where had Johnny gone to?
10 Hugo Kramer and Sergio Caporetti saw something on the table in front of them.
    (a) What were they looking at?
    (b) Why must they tell Benedict van der Byl immediately?

7

1   As soon as Benedict got the message from Kramer, he went to see Larsen.
    (a) What was Benedict going to do?
    (b) What reason did he give to Larsen?
    (c) What was the real reason?
2   'I want you to wait in my office,' Benedict told Ruby.
    (a) Where was Benedict going to go?
    (b) What did he tell Ruby to do?
3   'We dredged for sixty-six hours,' Johnny told them. What had he found?
4   'But it is not Larsen's decision,' said Benedict.
    (a) Who did Johnny now owe the money to?
    (b) What did Benedict want from Johnny?
    (c) How many days did Johnny have before he had to pay the interest?
5   Who came in when Benedict phoned? What did she tell Johnny?
6   Johnny went to a hotel. What did he do?
7   Who came to the room?
8   What did Johnny decide to do?

8

1   Benedict was angry – very angry.
    (a) Why did Benedict no longer want Ruby?
    (b) What did he tell Ruby to do?

2 'Have you forgotten about the computer?' Ruby asked slowly.
    (a) What did Ruby mean by this question?
    (b) What was Benedict's reply?
3 Ruby met Tracey at Johnny's hotel.
    (a) Where was Johnny?
    (b) What did Ruby tell Tracey?
4 How did Tracey get to Cartridge Bay?
5 What did Tracey tell Hugo Kramer?
6 'Where's Benedict van der Byl?' asked Kramer. What did Tracey reply?

9

1 Where was Benedict sitting? What had his father done there?
2 'Click! Click!' Benedict laughed.
    (a) Why did the gun not go off when Benedict pulled the trigger?
    (b) What did he do before he put the gun back on his father's desk?
3 What had Ruby come back to tell Benedict?
4 What did Benedict do as Ruby ran towards the door?
5 Where did Benedict throw the gun and the cartridges?
6 Why did Benedict want to get to Kramer and to *Wild Goose*?

10

1 Why was Sergio worried?
2 Johnny threw the computer reports onto the floor. What did he
   see lying on the table?
3 Johnny fed the program into the computer.
    (a) What was the name of the program?
    (b) What did Johnny and Tracey see on the screen?
4 What did Johnny remember?
5 Sergio took the bag of diamonds out of his desk. Where did he
   put the bag?
6 How did Sergio know that Johnny had found the Kaminikoto
   computer program?
7 Sergio raised the heavy metal handle. Then he stopped. Why?
8 What did Johnny find behind Kaminikoto's machine?
9 Johnny and Tracey were locked in the conveyor room.
    (a) Why could they not open the door to the cyclone room?
    (b) How could they see into the cyclone room?

11

1   Who was waiting for Kramer when *Wild Goose* got back to Cartridge Bay? What was he holding?

2   Where did Benedict want Kramer to take him? How much money did Kramer want before he took Benedict there?

3   How did Benedict and Kramer find out that Sergio was in charge of *Kingfisher*?

4   'We must get to *Kingfisher*,' said Kramer.
      (a) What did Kramer want to pick up from *Kingfisher*?
      (b) Why did Benedict want to go onto *Kingfisher*?

5   Benedict asked Sergio to give him the diamonds.
      (a) Where were the diamonds?
      (b) What was Sergio's reply?

6   What did Benedict tell Sergio to do?

7   What did Benedict do with the five crewmen?

8   Benedict went quickly to the cyclone room.
      (a) What did he do there?
      (b) How were Johnny and Tracey able to see him?

9   What would happen when the explosives went off in the cyclone room?

12

1   'You've killed them all!' shouted Sergio Caporetti. Why did Sergio think that Benedict had killed them?

2   'Look out! The bag!' shouted Caporetti.
      (a) What did Benedict do when he saw the bag of diamonds on the deck?
      (b) What did Caporetti do?
      (c) What happened next?

3   'Haven't you got the diamonds?' shouted Kramer.
      (a) What did Benedict reply?
      (b) What did Benedict mean by this reply?

4   At that moment, there was a loud crash. What had happened to *Wild Goose*?

5   What happened after the explosion in the cyclone room? How did Johnny and Tracey escape?

6   'My God! It's *Wild Goose!*' shouted Johnny.
     (a) Where was *Kingfisher* going?
     (b) What happened to *Wild Goose*?
7   What was Benedict holding onto with both hands?

13

1   Who sailed *Kingfisher* back to Cartridge Bay?
2   Why were the police waiting at Cartridge Bay?
3   Johnny asked Sergio what had happened to the diamonds.
4   'Two last questions,' the policeman said to Johnny.
     (a) What were the two questions?
     (b) What were Johnny's answers?
5   Why was Johnny going to the Red Gods?
6   Johnny checked the Land Rover carefully. Was everything in order?
7   Whose body did Johnny find at the Red Gods?
8   Why was Johnny sure that Benedict was alive?

14

1   There was a radio in the Land Rover. Why did Johnny not send a message to the police?
2   Johnny drove into the desert. What was he following?
3   How did Johnny know that Benedict was finished?
4   What did Johnny find in Benedict's jacket pocket?
5   Why was Johnny not able to go any further in the Land Rover?
6   How did Johnny know that he would find Benedict soon?
7   What was following Benedict?
8   What did Johnny see when he found Benedict?
9   Why could Johnny not kill Benedict?
10   'I'm going,' said Johnny.
     (a) Where were the hyenas?
     (b) What did Benedict say?
     (c) Did Johnny go?
11   How were the police able to find Johnny and Benedict?

GLOSSARY

Glossary

1 **lawyer** (page 7)
   a person who has studied law. People often need the help of a
   lawyer when they are writing their wills. (see Glossary no. 2)
2 **will** (page 7)
   a piece of paper on which you write who you want to have your
   money and your goods when you die.
3 **study** (page 7)
   a room in a house where you can sit quietly and read or write.
4 **debts** (page 9)
   the Van Der Byl Diamond Company has borrowed a lot of money
   from banks. The banks have lent the money to the company and
   these loans are now part of the company's debts. Sometimes a
   company has large debts which it cannot pay back to the bank.
   Then the bank can close the company and make it sell
   everything in order to pay its debts.
5 **whisper** (page 9)
   to speak very quietly.
6 **responsible** – *personally responsible* (page 9)
   if the banks close the Van Der Byl Diamond Company, Johnny
   Lance will have to pay all the company's debts himself.
7 **ruin** (page 9)
   to ruin someone is to take all their money from them and leave
   them without any money at all.
8 **rand** (page 9)
   money used in South Africa.
9 **concession** (page 10)
   land where the Van Der Byl Diamond Company has permission
   from the Government to look for diamonds.
10 **equipment** – *designed the equipment* (page 10)
   Johnny Lance has designed the equipment – drawn the plans for
   the machines and the computer which are on *Kingfisher*.
11 **off-shore** (page 11)
   the land which is under the sea on the sea-bed.
12 **coast** (page 11)
   where the sea and the land join together.

13 *gap* (page 11)

an open space between the two islands. The sea water can pass through the gap.

14 *marvellous* (page 12)

wonderful. Something which fills you with surprise.

15 *patrol* – *police patrol* (page 12)

diamonds are among the most valuable things in the world. Because they are so valuable, people steal them. Then they try to smuggle them – take them secretly – to Europe where they can sell them. The police patrols use planes to look for smugglers.

16 *pilchard* (page 12)

a small fish which is caught off the coast of South Africa. When the pilchards are caught, they are taken to a factory where they are cooked and put into cans with tomato sauce. Hugo Kramer is a fisherman, but he is also a diamond smuggler. He smuggles the diamonds out of South Africa by hiding them in the cans of pilchards.

17 *security officer* (page 14)

a security officer's job in a diamond mine is to stop people stealing diamonds.

18 *gas-filled* (page 14)

a gas-filled balloon is filled with a gas which is lighter than air. The balloon rises up in the sky and lifts the metal box up with it.

19 *radar screen* (page 14)

radar is an instrument on a ship which tells you where things are in the sea or sky around the ship. The screen on the radar is like a television screen.

20 *deck* (page 14)

the open part on top of a boat where you can stand and look out over the sea.

21 *cabin* (page 14)

a small room on a boat where you can sit or sleep.

22 *wax* – *hot wax* (page 14)

when you heat wax, it turns soft. When the wax is cold it becomes hard again. If Kramer put the diamonds into the can without the wax, they could move about and make a noise. The police might hear the noise and find the diamonds.

23 *divorce* (page 16)

a married couple can bring their marriage to an end by getting a divorce.

24 *briefcase* (page 17)
a case used for carrying books and papers.

25 *delighted* (page 17)
very pleased with something.

26 *safe* (page 17)
a metal box with a strong lock. You keep money and diamonds
and other valuable things in a safe.

27 *blonde* (page 19)
a woman with fair, light coloured hair.

28 **House** – *South Africa House* (page 22)
the embassy of South Africa in London.

29 *fields* – *underwater diamond fields* (page 22)
a diamond field is ground where you can find diamonds. An
underwater diamond field is the ground on the sea-bed where you
can find diamonds.

30 *dredging* (page 22)
to dredge is to dig up the mud and sand on the sea-bed and lift it
up from the bottom of the sea onto a boat.

31 *computer expert* (page 23)
someone who knows a lot about computers.

32 *conveyor belt* (page 23)
to convey something is to move it from one place to another. A
conveyor belt is a long piece of strong cloth or plastic. The belt is
moved round and round by machinery. As the belt moves,
anything placed on it is carried from one end to the other. The
conveyor belt on *Kingfisher* is inside a long tunnel.

33 *x-ray* (page 23)
an instrument which lets you see the inside of things. If any
diamonds are found, they will be seen on the screen of the x-ray
machine.

34 *graded* (page 23)
to grade diamonds is to put them in the order of their value. The
best diamonds are put together, then the next best, and so on.

35 *hatch* – *inspection hatch* (page 24)
a hatch is an opening like a small door. You open an inspection
hatch and climb through it to look at the machinery inside.

36 *anchor* (page 27)
when a ship wants to stay in one place out at sea, it drops an
anchor – a heavy weight – over the side. The anchor is fixed to
the ship by a long, thick wire – the anchor cable.

37 **program** (page 27)
a computer program tells the computer what to do.

38 **dredge head** (page 27)
the dredge head is at the front of the dredging machine. It is the part of the machine which cuts into the mud and sand and rocks on the sea-bed.

39 **Board Meeting** (page 30)
the directors of a company are the people at the top of the company who make all the important decisions. A meeting of directors to make decisions is called a Board Meeting. The Board of Directors meet in a special room called the Board Room.

40 **interest** (page 31)
extra money which you have to pay when you borrow money from a bank.

41 **share** (page 31)
each share in a company is worth a certain amount of money. If a company is doing well, each share is worth a lot of money. The Van Der Byl Diamond Company is in debt so the shares are not worth any money at the moment. But they will be worth a lot of money when people learn that many large diamonds have been found at Thunderbolt and Suicide.

42 **charter** (page 34)
to rent or hire a plane.

43 **landing strip** (page 35)
a flat piece of land where a plane can land safely.

44 **trigger** (page 36)
you load a gun by putting in a cartridge. When you want to fire the loaded gun, you pull the trigger with your finger.

45 **cyclone room** (page 42)
the room on *Kingfisher* where the mud and sand and stones is turned round and round at very high speed. All the water is thrown out and goes back into the sea. Only the mud and sand and stones are left.

46 **in charge** (page 45)
Caporetti is in charge – in control – of *Kingfisher*. When you are in charge, people have to do what you tell them to do.

47 **explosive** – *plastic explosive* (page 47)
a bomb is filled with explosives. Plastic explosives are soft and can be put round pipes. A timer works like a clock and is fixed to the plastic explosive. When the hand of the timer moves to a fixed time, there is a powerful explosion.

48 **hanged** (page 50)

in South Africa, criminals who commit murder are put to death. A rope is fixed round the neck of the criminal. A hole opens in the floor under the prisoner's feet and he is left hanging from the rope. His neck is broken and he dies.

49 **propeller** (page 50)

a propeller is fixed to the back of a ship. The ship's engine makes the propeller turn round and round. As the propeller turns round, it pushes the ship forward.

50 **raft** – *rubber raft* (page 53)

a rubber raft is a small boat which floats on the water. If a ship sinks, people jump off the ship and get into the raft.

51 **current** (page 55)

a current is the movement of the water in the sea.

52 **kit** – *first-aid kit* (page 55)

a small box in which you keep the things you need if you have an accident.

53 **hyena** (page 55)

a wild animal. A hyena will attack humans if they are weak or injured.

54 **flare** – *smoke flare* (page 60)

when you put a lighted match to a smoke flare, it burns and gives out a cloud of red smoke. The red smoke can be seen from far away so the police are able to see where Johnny and Benedict are.

Shane *by Jack Schaefer*
Old Mali and the Boy *by D. R. Sherman*
Bristol Murder *by Philip Prowse*
Tales of Goha *by Leslie Caplan*
The Smuggler *by Piers Plowright*
The Pearl *by John Steinbeck*
Things Fall Apart *by Chinua Achebe*
The Woman Who Disappeared *by Philip Prowse*
The Moon is Down *by John Steinbeck*
A Town Like Alice *by Nevil Shute*
The Queen of Death *by John Milne*
Walkabout *by James Vance Marshall*
Meet Me in Istanbul *by Richard Chisholm*
The Great Gatsby *by F. Scott Fitzgerald*
The Space Invaders *by Geoffrey Matthews*
My Cousin Rachel *by Daphne du Maurier*
I'm the King of the Castle *by Susan Hill*
Dracula *by Bram Stoker*
The Sign of Four *by Sir Arthur Conan Doyle*
The Speckled Band and Other Stories by *Sir Arthur Conan Doyle*
The Eye of the Tiger *by Wilbur Smith*
The Queen of Spades and Other Stories *by Aleksandr Pushkin*
The Diamond Hunters *by Wilbur Smith*
When Rain Clouds Gather *by Bessie Head*
Banker *by Dick Francis*
No Longer at Ease *by Chinua Achebe*
The Franchise Affair *by Josephine Tey*
The Case of the Lonely Lady *by John Milne*

For further information on the full selection of
Readers at all five levels in the series, please refer
to the Heinemann ELT Readers catalogue.

Macmillan Heinemann English Language Teaching
Between Towns Road, Oxford OX4 3PP
A division of Macmillan Publishers Limited
Companies and representatives throughout the world

ISBN 0 435 27231 4

Heinemann is a registered trade mark of Reed Educational and Professional Publishing Ltd

© Wilbur A. Smith 1971
First Published by William Heinemann Ltd 1971
This retold version for Heinemann ELT Guided Readers
© Margaret Tarner 1989, 1992
First published 1989
This edition published 1992

Illustrated by Trevor Ridley
Typography by Adrian Hodgkins
Cover by Chris Vine and Threefold Design
Typeset in 11/12.5 pt Goudy
by Joshua Associates Ltd, Oxford
Printed and bound in Spain by Mateu Cromo, S.A.

2004 2003 2002 2001 2000
16 15 14 13 12 11 10 9 8 7